For Rafe
M.B.

For John
C.R.

First published in Great Britain 2023 by Walker Books Ltd
87 Vauxhall Walk, London SE11 5HJ

2 4 6 8 10 9 7 5 3 1

Text © 2023 Mac Barnett
Illustrations © 2023 Christian Robinson

The right of Mac Barnett and Christian Robinson to be identified as author and illustrator respectively of this work
has been asserted in accordance with the Copyright, Designs and Patents Act 1988

This book has been typeset in Avenir

Printed in China

British Library Cataloguing in Publication Data:
a catalogue record for this book is
available from the British Library

ISBN 978-1-5295-1278-6

www.walker.co.uk

Twenty Questions

MAC BARNETT   CHRISTIAN ROBINSON

WALKER BOOKS
AND SUBSIDIARIES
LONDON • BOSTON • SYDNEY • AUCKLAND

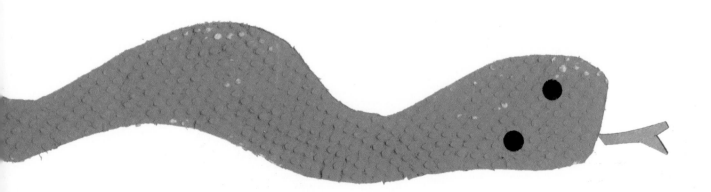

How many animals can you see in this picture?

How many animals can you not see in this one, because they're hiding from the tiger?

Which of these ladies just robbed a bank?

Why is the elephant so upset?

What is this boy hiding
behind his back?

How did that cow get all the way up there?

Where did the bandits
bury the treasure?

What would you do
if you found it?

Which
of these
creatures
is the
zookeeper's
favourite?

Who gave Mr Beckett
a bump on his noggin?

What did the lion
get the lamb
for her birthday?

Who is she waiting for?

Which of these fellows has a better singing voice?

What
kind of
beast
lives
in this
bathtub?

And what does it eat?

Who is on the other side of this door?

Which of these children is dreaming of peaches?

Where is this ship sailing away to?

Will you go with it?

Are you ever coming back?

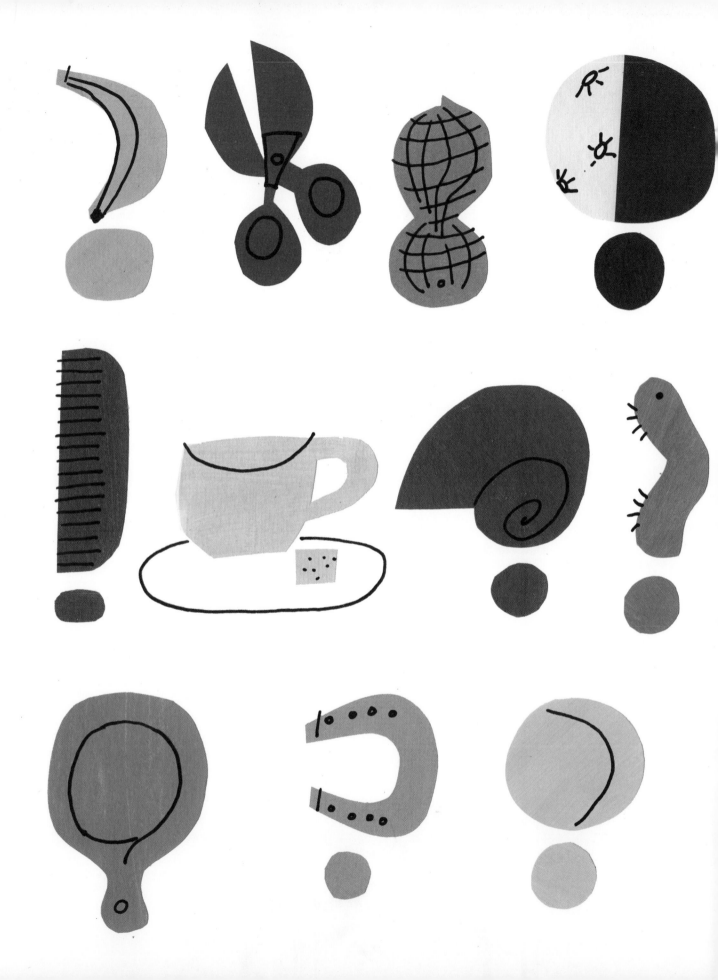